INTRODUCTION

Dear reader,

 I am presenting this book on the girl who is usually very unhappy with certain stages of her life. As we all know god does not gives everything to everyone and some people are never satisfied with what they get while some are too much satisfied. God examines them, whether they can face problems or not? Same happens with the girl

whom I described in
my book.

CONTENTS

UNDERESTIMAT
ED HER......

3) WHEN SHE WAS
FAILED......

4) WHEN SHE
FINALLY
BECOMES HAPPY

FROM

UNHAPPY....

PART

1:

WHEN TARA'S FRIEND LEFT HER...

There was a 9 years
old girl named 'Tara' ,
she lived very happily
with

her family . She was
unaware of all the
affliction which are
going to

come in her life in this
very tender age. One
day when she went

school, she saw other
girl sitting on her desk
beside her friend. She

was very upset after
seeing that. She sat on

another place
unhappily.

She was waiting for
the lunch break so that
she could talk to her

friend. She cannot
concentrate on what
the teacher is teaching

because of what she had seen. Finally the bell for lunch break rang ,

and she went to her best friend 'Sameeksha'. When she asked her

why she allowed that
other girl to sit beside
her , Sameeksha
replied

that she was bored of
Tara and wants to
make a new friend,
because

Tara didn't have good looks and she don't like making fun during

class. Tara was very unhappy after listening that, she never thought

that her best friend
behave so bad with
her. She went home
and

cried a lot , when her
mother asked what
happened she didn't
told

anything and silently
went into her room. At
evening, she went to

Sameeksha's home. And
again asked her why
she thinks so about her

she told her that her
mother and sister
suggested her to make

another friend as she
feels ashamed with her
because of her(Tara's)

looks. Tara came back
to her home. And told
everything to her

mother. Her mother
explained her not to be
unhappy and stay

satisfied with
whatever she have got.
Her mother also told
her not

not to worry because
looks never matters, a
person should have to

be kind from heart,
and she was very sure
that one day she will
get a

good friend. Tara went
to sleep. She was still
very unconscious

because she was too
little to face such
things in her life. Her
mother

was also very shocked
that how someone
could think like that
for a

person at very small
age. When she waked
up her mother told her
to

get ready for her
school. She went

school but still was
unhappy. Her

teacher scolded her as
she was constantly
looking at Sameeksha
and

Riya. When her
teacher contacted her
mother , then only her

Teacher could
understood the reason
behind such behavior
of Tara.

When Tara was eating her lunch , Riya went from her side she

pushed her slightly by saying , " So now madam is eating her lunch".

Tara said nothing and
went to wash her
hands. She met
Sameeksha

there she looked
Sameeksha for a while
and than went to
classroom

by ignoring her.
Sameeksha ran
towards the classroom
, she pushed

Tara and shouted on
her why she looked at
her. She said that Tara

had spoiled her day by looking at her. Tara was very shocked. Really

this was a terrifying condition for a little girl in 4th standard. This

was the first and worst
storm like situation
that Tara had to face.

"GOOD
LOOKS
FADES
AWAY BUT
GOOD
HEART
KEEPS

YOU
BEAUTIFUL
FOREVER."

PART 2:

WHEN

EVERYBOY

UNDERESTI MATED HER...

As Sameeksha never liked her looks , no student in the class likes to

be with Tara because
Sameeksha is the most
beautiful girl of the

class as well as the
class monitor. But
Tara is more intelligent
than

Sameeksha. But no one cares that, they just cares the bad looks of

Tara. They always laughed on Tara by say "Ugly Tara, Ugly Tara".

We can't imagine what
the condition of the
little girl was because

she was facing an
extreme worst
condition of getting
ignored. Colour

discrimination is one of the most bad thing that some peoples even

kids also practices in our society. Today is Tara's birthday. She was

going to become 14
years old. She invited
her classmates by

forgetting what they
did with her because
Tara is very kind
person

she never hated them.
She was just unhappy.
But none of her

classmates came
because they hated
Tara. Tara cried a lot.
She

asked god " Did I even
not have a right to
celebrate the most
special

day of my life just
because of my looks?"
She was very
disappointed.

She was very nervous.
She was very unhappy.
What is her fault?

Is to look normal was
her fault? OR Ignoring
fun during class was
her fault?

Why people don't see
her kind behavior?
Why Sameeksha was

getting special attention? Just because of that worst thinking of

Good and Bad looks. One day a new teacher after completing lesson told

them a joke. Everybody
laughed instead of
Tara because she was

completing her work.
Everyone pointed
towards Tara and said ,

"see how she is studying, like she was going to be the topper of the

world". The teacher scolded Tara to not listen what she was telling

to all of them. Tara
was not able to
understand why the
teacher

appreciated the other
students. She don't
knows that the teacher

is also attracted to the good looking Sameeksha. She was surprised

with the underestimating behavior of everyone towards her. She

went home and went to her bedroom. She

cried a lot. She got
tired

what was happening
with her daily. She
realizes that she was
alone

, nobody is with her.
This was the second

storm like situation that

too make Tara depressed.

"BEING UNDERESTI MATED IS

ONE OF
THE
BIGGEST
COMPETITI
VE
ADVANTAG
ES YOU
CAN HAVE."

SO PUSH
UP
YOURSELF.

PART 3:

WHEN SHE WAS FAILED...

Tara was totally depressed of whatever happened with her.

Her exams are going to
come but she can't
concentrate on her

studies. She knows
that if she don't
concentrate she will

fail. Finally her exams
came. She gave the
exams. Slowly , slowly

days goes on. She was
very worried that what
will be the results of

her exams. Because
this time she was not
confident as always

she was about her
exams. Finally the
result came. She got A
grade

in exams. The result
was not satisfying for
her because she always

gets A++ grade.
According to her she
failed in achieving her
target.

Her mother told her
not to worry and do
her best next time.
But

she was totally
depressed. Her
friends, her teachers,
her

classmates, her luck,
nothing of them is with
her. Now it was

the only situation when she felt to be failed in her life. We can't

describe the condition of Tara. It seems that God is examining

her a lot. She even thought to commit

suicide and tried too but

did not succeed in doing so. She never thought that one day

she had to face such type of situation. She was truly an

unhappy girl. She had
faced the third and
most devastating

situation of her life in
form of failure.

"FAILURE
IS

NOTHING MORE THAN A CHANCE TO REVISE YOUR

STRATEGY
"
.

PART 4:

WHEN SHE FINALLY

BECOMES HAPPY FROM UNHAPPY...

One day a new girl
named Janhvi joined

her class . When
Janhvi seen

Tara sitting alone. She
requested Tara to join
her. Tara don't knows

That Janhvi is the one
whom she needs,

Janhvi is the one who
can

bring happiness to her
life. Janhvi was totally
impressed with her

she always clapped for
Tara when she gives

any speech or gets
award

Janhvi was like a fairy
of Tara' s life. After a
long time Tara had

smiled, laughed and
enjoyed. Janhvi has
become an important

part of Tara's life. Today is the most important and happiest day

of Tara's life. She ranked good in her medical exams. After

completing training she
finally achieved her
goal by becoming

a doctor. Janhvi
congratulated her.
Tara told Janhvi about

whatever she thinks
about her. Janhvi was

very happy to know
that.

They both are made
for each other. Finally
Tara got her true best

friend. Finally our
"UNHAPPY" girl

becomes very very
much "HAPPY".

"HAPPIN
ESS IS
LETTING
GO OF
WHAT
YOU THINK

YOUR LIFE IS SUPPOSE D TO LOOK LIKE."

SO JUST
REMOV
E "UN"
FROM

“UNHAPPY
”, YOU
WILL
AUTOMATI
CALLY
FIND THE
WAY TO

BE
"HAPPY".

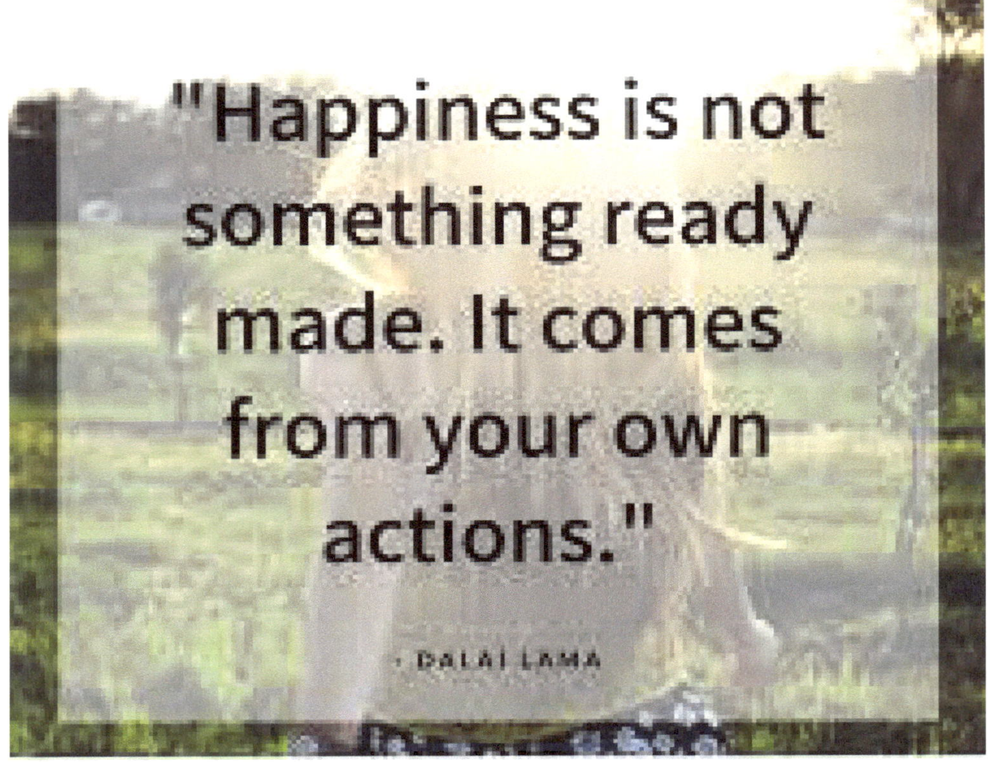

KeepInspiring.me

"Spread love
everywhere you go.
Let no one ever
come without
leaving happier."

MOTHER TERESA

GH

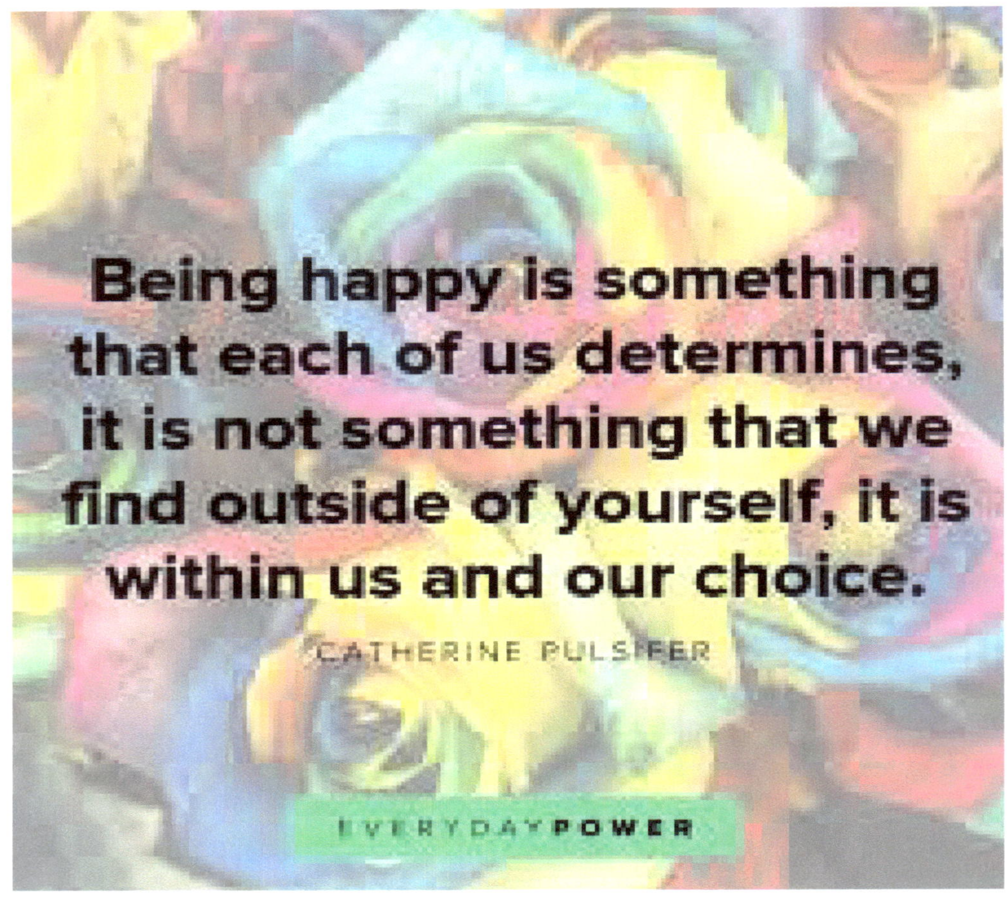

Being happy is something that each of us determines, it is not something that we find outside of yourself, it is within us and our choice.

CATHERINE PULSIFER

EVERYDAYPOWER

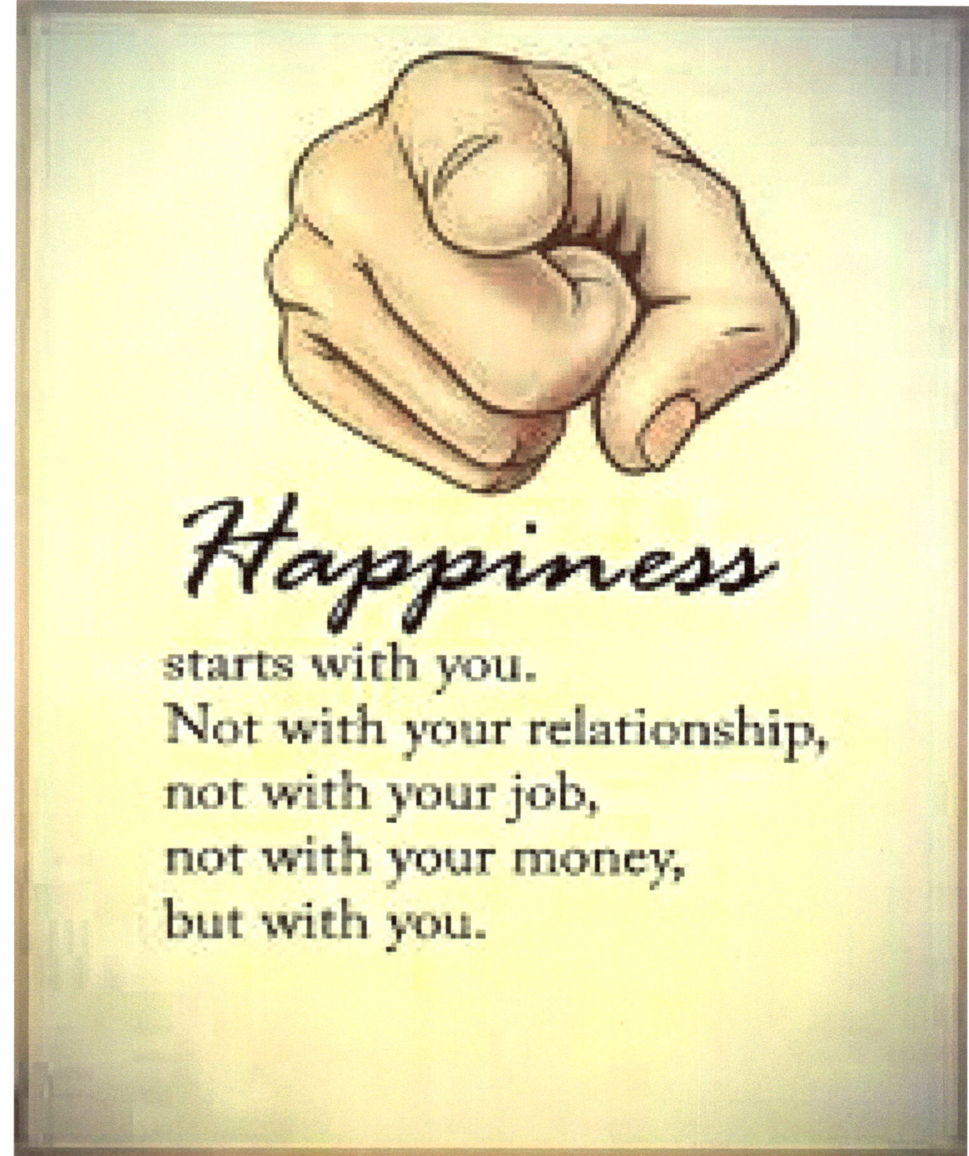
Happiness
starts with you.
Not with your relationship,
not with your job,
not with your money,
but with you.

"Being Happy
Never Goes
Out of Style"
Lilly Pulitzer

Be happy ...
not because
everything is good,
but because you
can see the good
in everything
WARWICK
International Hotels

I'm just a girl

I love being called pretty, but I'll never believe it.
I'm not always right, but hate admitting I'm wrong.
I'm almost always smiling, but it's not always real.
I can be read like an open book, but hide so much.
I work hard at things, but don't always get what I deserve.

I'm just a girl

KEYS TO HAPPINESS
HAPPINESS NEVER DECREASES BY BEING SHARED
HAPPINESS ALWAYS SNEAKS IN A DOOR YOU DID NOT THINK WAS OPEN
HAPPINESS IS A CHOICE. CHOOSE HAPPY!
SUCCESS IS NOT THE KEY TO HAPPINESS. HAPPINESS IS THE KEY TO SUCCESS
DON'T PUT THE KEY TO YOUR HAPPINESS IN SOMEONE ELSE'S POCKET
DON'T WORRY, BE HAPPY!
NEVER LET ANYONE STEAL YOUR HAPPINESS
HAPPINESS IS ALWAYS A CHOICE, WHATEVER YOUR RELATIONSHIP STATUS
HAPPINESS IS NOT A DESTINATION. IT IS A METHOD OF LIFE
www.shutterstock.com • 673627003

Happiness does not have
a price tag
so smile.
-Jade Lebea

7 Steps to Happiness:

Think Less, Feel More

Frown Less, Smile More

Talk Less, Listen more

Judge Less, Accept More

Watch Less, Do More

Complain Less, Appreciate More

Fear Less, Love More

THANKS

FOR READING

HOPE

YOU

LIKED

IT